The Saddest Dragon

By Joshua Eastman

Edited by Ruth Eastman

Creative Design by Daniella & Yoni Eastman

ISBN: 9798838426697

DEDICATION

Thank you to G-d for making this all possible.

Thank you to my wife Sima for being the wind beneath my wings in all things.

Thank you to my mother Ruth who edited both the grammar and the content.

And finally, thank you to Daniella and Yoni – you are the reason this story exists, and I am so very grateful you let me tell it to you so many times. Thank you for being a very regal Princess Adelaide and a thoroughly fearsome Dragon!

And thank you for letting me be your very proud dad!

There once was a princess named Adelaide who lived in the magical kingdom of Carf Melys, a wondrous land filled with light and joy.

Adelaide was no ordinary princess. She was smart, and brave, and kind, and always curious. What made her extra special is she was kind to everyone and everything, which even the best princesses sometimes forget or have to learn on the job. What also set her apart from other princesses was her curiosity and need to know new things. She was an inventor, always trying new things and finding ways to solve all problems she could. Sometimes, it worked great! Other times, well… After those times she would help clean up the mess her invention inevitably caused and she would say, "Back to the old drawing board!" and go right back to inventing something better.

It was one fine sunny day in the long Carf Melys summer, and Adelaide was out in the castle gardens, exploring the flower beds for signs of Fairies. They liked to eat all the flowers of the growing plants, and that wouldn't do at all! So, Adelaide was hoping to give them something even better. With the help of Royal Chef Esmund, she had made several cakes that were filled with sweets fairies like even more than flowers. She was putting the last of them in the flowerbed when she heard yelling from beyond the gate. Being as curious as she was, she quickly ran to the gate and looked toward the nearby forest.

Running up the road from the forest came one of her father's knights. She could tell who he was right away. Sir Reginald Sir of the Sirrington Sirs, a family filled with brave knights who all served the king of Carf Melys. Adelaide was surprised to see him running and shouting like that. Something must have really scared the brave knight! She listened to hear what he was saying, and the other people who had been outside did the same. Sir Sir, out of breath and yet somehow still able to shout (something he was very proud of, by the way), was yelling "Dragon! There's a dragon in the forest!" He reached the group of people who had come out to see him, and he stopped, took a huge gulp of air, and quickly explained.

"I was in the forest picking mushrooms for a late lunch, when I bumped straight into a wall! Now, I knew there couldn't be a wall in a forest -- we Sirs of Sirrington being as smart as we are -- and yet there was a wall. A wall! In the woods! Figuring it to be enchanted, and possibly a magic wall with a magic door in it, I began to look up. And then, I noticed it wasn't a wall at all. It was the leg of a MASSIVE DRAGON!"

Here, he stretched his arms out wide. “It had to have been this...well, I can’t really show you but bigger than this!” Not figuring that to be dramatic enough, he said, “Much much **MUCH BIGGER** than this!”

Everyone gasped, except for Adelaide. “A dragon,” she thought. “A dragon! I’ve never seen a dragon!”

Sir Sir continued, “He has teeth as long as our swords! Claws as big as my head! His roar nearly knocked me off my feet!”

One of the onlookers leaned in, looking worried. “But, did he burn you with his fiery breath?”

Sir Sir paused in the middle of waving his arms dramatically and looked in confusion at the questioner. "I -- I don't know. I feel as if he had I'd have known about it, but who knows? I ran out of those woods so fast I didn't even have time to think about it!" He pointed at the castle. "Either way, burned or no, I'm not going back in there until the king can bring all the knights out to protect us from this terrible menace!" So saying, he continued running in through the castle gates, through the gardens, and up the castle steps to the king's throne room.

Adelaide was a brave and curious girl, which we said at the beginning of our story. I should mention that because of these traits, she was fearless as well. Certainly, a dragon would be an amazing sight to see! She was so curious that she decided to go right then and see this dragon for herself. She walked down the path from the castle to the forest, and headed right in.

Now being a magical kingdom, the land was magical as well. The forest, being very near the center of the whole kingdom, was the most magical part of all. Parts of the forest that looked small suddenly looked bigger when you walked through them; parts that seemed huge would shrink; and sometimes trees would change places for no apparent reason at all. Some of the villagers in the town from the far side of the forest would tell stories of trees dancing around all night long to music only the oldest villagers could hear. It was very rare to find trees lying down in this forest, but after a hard night of dancing and playing, who could blame the ones that did?

Adelaide wandered through the sunlit forest, heading toward the faint roaring she heard in the distance. She listened as the trees whispered back and forth to each other which was surprising not because magical trees could speak, but BECAUSE they were magical, she kind of expected them to speak about mystical, wondrous things. Instead they spoke of the same things she might: the weather; who wore what to which forest dance; what they were having for dinner... Adelaide just smiled and shook her head. She continued down the trail.

She walked and walked and walked, and just when she'd begun to think maybe there was no dragon at all, and maybe it was time for supper, she rounded a bend -- and sitting in the middle of a large clearing was a gigantic red-scaled dragon. He wasn't paying attention to her at all, for he was instead busy staring at a nearby rock. She was surprised at how big the dragon was. But Adelaide was a princess, and as far as she knew princesses were afraid of nothing, so she wasn't scared even a little bit.

The dragon was taking deep breaths in, as if he was trying to suck in all the air in the entire world. And then he blew out all the air at once, directing the full fury of his powerful lungs on the rock in front of him. Like most rocks however, this rock remained unimpressed and unmoving. Rocks found very few things worth getting up and moving about for, and a dragon wasn't typically one of them. And this rock came from a very illustrious and stolid family of rocks and was particularly uninterested in changing that now. The dragon's shoulders slumped, and he sighed.

Adelaide said, “Excuse me, Mister Dragon,” for she was very polite indeed. The startled dragon turned quickly in her direction. When he saw the princess, he let loose a mighty roar that shook the trees. He raised his huge arms and wings to their full height in the air.

“RRRROOOOOOOOOOOOOOAAAAAAAAAAAAAARRRRRRRRRR!!!” The dragon said, and then when he saw she had not moved, he began another terrifying roar.

"RRRROOOAAAAARRR -- oh, what's the point?" He stopped in the middle, lowered his wings and his head, and began to cry. Great big dragon tears came gushing out, and Adelaide had to dodge them for fear they would wash her away! His sobbing startled the rock, finally, which being from a stolid family of rocks was uncomfortable around crying things, and the rock quickly scuttled off into the forest, muttering to himself grumpily. Rocks did hate moving almost as much as they hated being moved, after all.

The Saddest Dragon

Adelaide was a very kind spirit, and as we've said before, very, very brave. She approached the weeping dragon and placed a hand on his scaly leg. He glanced down at her through his fingers, and again he looked surprised to see her still there. "Aren't you afraid, little girl?"

She frowned. "Are *you* afraid, Mister Dragon? And by the way -- my parents tell me I am tall for my age. I'm not little."

The dragon shifted slightly to see her better. "Um. Well, everyone is little to me, except other dragons, of course." He squinted slightly and sniffled. "But why didn't you run away? That was my most *terrifying* roar!"

She smiled at him. “My father the king snores at night so loudly, I can hear him from across the castle. I’m not afraid anyway, because I am a princess.”

The dragon thought about that, but as dragons don’t have school like most children, all they learn comes from experience, and this was his first meeting with a princess. So, in the absence of any other information, the dragon supposed she could be correct. He nodded sagely, not wanting her to know he had no idea. “Yes, Yes, I’ve heard that princesses are afraid of nothing. Because I’ve met lots and lots of princesses on my travels. Yes, maybe millions of princesses.”

Adelaide doubted that, as she *was* in school, and she was sure that not many princesses would have come up to visit the dragon in the forest. But that wasn't what drew her attention at the time. She saw how sad the dragon was, and she realized suddenly that she had no idea why.

"Mister Dragon, what's wrong? Why are you so sad?" He started to tear up again, so Adelaide quickly dove behind a tree just as the first gigantic tear hit the ground.

"I'm...I'm...not very good at being a dragon," the dragon cried. "None of the other dragons like me or want to play with me because I can't breathe fire."

He hung his head. "Whenever all the dragon families gather, they hold contests about who can shoot their fire the farthest, or who can burn the most rocks; but me, they just laugh at me because I can't blow fire even a little."

He started crying even more, and the ground shook as he sobbed into his big clawed hands. Adelaide said, "But surely you can make friends with other creatures besides dragons? Can't you?"

He looked at her sadly. "People don't like dragons, because we're too big to fit in houses, and it's hard for us to hold teacups, and there's also the fire thing. And honestly, dragons tend to stick with other dragons for the same reasons. It's just easier."

Adelaide smiled brightly. "Well, I can be your friend!"

The dragon just sobbed harder at that. "You are very kind, Princess; but I'm afraid I don't know how to be friends with people. It's just so easy to squish them by accident! And if you squish even one, they get upset. I hate when people are upset with me. It's just easier to be alone. And until I can breathe fire, I can't have any dragon friends either. No Princess, I'm afraid I'll never have friends." And with that, he crawled off into the woods, tail drooping behind him.

Adelaide thought about following him, but it was getting very late and the sun was starting to set. The clouds were pink in the sky, and she knew that meant soon it would be time for dinner and bed, and she didn't want to miss that! She hurried home, thinking all the while about the poor, sad dragon in the woods. If only there were some way that she could help him! She hurried back into the castle and up the stairs just in time to see her father eating dinner at the table.

"Father, oh Father, I have a question for you! I saw the dragon today, the dragon in the forest, and he can't breathe fire so he's sad, and I want to help him, but I don't know how! Can we please help him?"

The king looked at his daughter for a moment before he spoke. “You saw the dragon? Adelaide, you should not have run off without seeing me first. It’s lucky the trees saw you and told us where you’d gone, or we might have been worried. I’ve already spoken with Sir Sir, and when he calmed down enough to explain what happened, I knew the dragon you had met wasn’t dangerous to you. After all, it scared off Sir Sir, when it could have just as easily eaten him whole!” He came around the table and gave Adelaide a hug. “But my darling brave princess, you must still tell your mother or me what you’re doing, all right? Besides, did you ask your dear old dad if maybe he also wanted to see a dragon?”

Adelaide looked up at him and saw him smiling. She was glad not to be in trouble. It simply hadn't occurred to her, but she knew she'd remember in the future. Still, she really wanted to help the dragon. "He says all the other dragons make fun of him because he can't breathe fire. How can I help him? I want him to not be sad, because I don't think anyone should be that sad."

The king's smile widened. "You have a good heart, Princess. And you are an inventor. What if you thought of something besides fire that could help him with the other dragons?"

Adelaide smiled back at him. "You're right, Father! I just have to think of something he could do with what he already has!"

She raced off, and the king chuckled to himself before carrying her forgotten dinner to her room so it wouldn't get too cold before she ate it.

Adelaide sat in the garden near the forest the next morning, lost in thought. If only she could find a way to help that poor, sad dragon! She wandered back and forth, carefully stepping over the fairies dragging the treats she had left them into the woods. Sir Archibald Sir, cousin of Sir Reginald Sir, and part of the Sirringderry Sirs, went striding past, carrying a large tub filled with soap. "Good morning, lass!" He shouted and waved. It seems he had forgotten about the tub of soap, as by waving, he had taken his hand off the side and the whole tub flipped over, covering him with soap.

Adelaide laughed as he spluttered and said some very unknightly words. She offered him a kerchief. “Good morning, Sir Sir!”

He took the offered token and began swiping at the soap. As he turned about, trying to brush at the soap, bubbles flew off him into the surrounding air. Realizing what he probably looked like, Sir Sir began to laugh as well, and turned his soap removal into a brief jig, dancing in a very funny fashion indeed.

Adelaide laughed and clapped in time, until she was struck by an idea. Well, until she was struck by a *bubble* -- but it was as the bubble struck that she had the idea.

"Sir Sir? Can you get your cousin Sir Sir, and maybe his brother Sir Sir, and maybe your uncle Sir Sir to help me out with an idea? I think I know how to help the dragon to be happy!"

Sir Sir bowed deeply, and bubbles flew into the air as he did so. "Of Course, Milady. The knights of Sirrington and Sirringderry stand ready to assist you on any valiant quest!" He paused thoughtfully. "As long as lunch is somehow involved?" He waited hopefully.

She nodded. "Of course, Sir Sir! I shall pack the finest picnic the kingdom has ever known!" And she quickly outlined her plan to the knight.

By midday, they had managed to find the wagon Adelaide had requested, along with the supplies she needed for her plan to work. As the knights helped her drive the wagon, she was able to travel quickly, and very soon they reached the clearing where she had last seen the dragon. When they arrived, she called out, “Mister Dragon, it is I, the princess you met yesterday! I think I have found something to help you!”

The trees bent back as the dragon came loping back into the center of the clearing. He still looked sad, but there was hope in his eyes as he said, “You found a way for me to breathe fire?”

Adelaide shook her head no. The dragon started to cry again, but she quickly reached into the wagon and pulled out a metal hoop from a barrel. "Here! This is the first part." She had to hold the hoop with both hands, but the dragon reached down and picked it up between two fingers, and when he held it looked like a tiny ring. Adelaide then had the knights drag over the tub of soap she had brought with her as well.

The dragon watched all this curiously, until he no longer could bear the mystery. "Princess, what is this?"

Sir Archibald Sir looked up at him and said, “Well, I suppose a dragon doesn’t take very many baths or wash their clothes, since your suit is a part of your body.”

Adelaide spoke up quickly. “What Sir Sir *means* to say is not that you don’t take baths in a bathtub. You probably use lakes or oceans instead, right?”

The dragon glowered briefly at Sir Sir before turning to the princess. “Is that what you brought me? A bathtub for really small creatures? I’m not sure how that will help.”

"Why, no!" exclaimed Adelaide. "This is a most magical creation of our kingdom. It's called 'soap.' Just watch what you can do with it." She opened a small case she had brought from the wagon and pulled out a beautiful golden bubble-blower. She dipped it in the soap, gave the bubble-blower a quick shake, took a deep breath, and blew. From the bubble-blower, a handful of small rainbow bubbles gently flew into the air, shining and popping like tiny diamonds in the sun.

The dragon's eyes got huge, and he looked at the ring he was holding. "Can I try?"

Adelaide took a break from bubble-blowing and smiled up at him. "That's the idea!"

The dragon reached down and submerged the hoop in the soapy water. Giving it a quick shake as he had seen the princess do, he brought the hoop up to his mouth. Drawing in breath the same way he had yesterday, he breathed out. There was no fire, for that was not something he could do. Instead, his mighty dragon breath filled the air with bubbles from the hoop.

And what bubbles they were! There were bubbles as big as houses, bubbles inside other bubbles, bubbles shaped like animals, bubbles that sang and bubbles that made other bubbles as they flew. Adelaide and the knights *oohed* and *aahed* like it was a show. And slowly but surely, the dragon started to smile. And soon after that, he was roaring with laughter.

The whole clearing shook with his laughter, and the bubbles filled the air. For while he couldn't breathe fire, the dragon could make amazing bubbles!

As Adelaide joined the dragon in making bubbles, a terrific sound filled the air. A heavy roaring filled the sky above her, mixed with the sounds of huge flapping wings. Adelaide looked up just in time to see dozens of dragons flying in the air above the clearing, staring at the bubbles. The dragons were magnificent, hued in brilliant colors from all throughout the rainbow, and they were all sizes as well. She watched as they landed all around the clearing and watched the dragon blowing bubbles.

A large gray dragon leaned in, fire curling around his mouth like a mustache. He poked a bubble with a long claw, and then sniffed the air. His voice was very loud, and the other dragons got quiet as he spoke. "How are you doing this...magic?"

The other dragons all nodded and turned expectantly to the once sad but now happy dragon, who offered the hoop to the grey dragon. "Do you want to try? It's human magic, but it's really easy to do!"

The gray dragon grasped the hoop, filled it with soap, but when he breathed out, fire roared from his mouth, singeing several nearby treetops and popping all the bubbles nearby. The gray dragon tried again, but again the fire ruined the bubbles before they could fly. He stomped off in a huff. One by one, the other dragons tried to blow bubbles. Not a single one could do it, for every time they breathed out, the bubbles popped in the fire. A small blue dragon burst into tears. “We can’t do it!” He wailed.

The happy dragon leaned back in and took the hoop. "Don't worry, I can make many more bubbles for us to play with." All the other dragons gathered around him, and he began to blow bubbles so huge that some of the dragons were caught up in them and lifted up into the sky. The dragons began to laugh and cheer. Soon, the saddest dragon with no friends at all became the happiest dragon. All the other dragons marveled at his magic and begged his forgiveness, desperate as they were to be his friend. Adelaide watched and clapped and laughed along with the dragons for hours and hours, but soon the sun started to go down again, and she knew it was time to go.

The happiest dragon came over to her as she got back into the wagon and bent down to see her off. Smiling a huge dragon smile, he thanked her. "Princess, you've given me friends and magic, and shown me that all I ever needed was to use my weakness as my strength, to not worry about being the best *dragon* but to be the best **me**. I don't know if I can ever repay you!"

Adelaide reached out and hugged the dragon's nose. "What else are friends for? I only ask one thing."

The dragon nodded. "Anything! Anything at all!"

Adelaide smiled. "Can I come to play again tomorrow?"

The dragon laughed and said, "Of course! And bring your friends as well!" They said their goodbyes, and the Sirs of Sirrington and Sirringderry waved to the other dragons and they were off for the castle. They got home just in time for dinner.

They say even now, if you listen carefully at the edge of a forest (as most of them are magical anywhere you are), you can hear the trees talking about the happiest dragon in the woods. And some people say you can even still hear the dragon's booming laugh and see every now and then a giant bubble rise into the air. But there is one thing everyone agrees on. From that day on, the saddest dragon was never sad again.

THE END

Afterword

Thank you for reading our story. It means a lot to all of us, Because it has been near and dear to our hearts for a long time, and we are so happy to get to share it with you. The woods of Carf Melys are chock-full of other tales yet to be told, so I would keep an eye out if I were you – Princess Adelaide will be back for more brave adventures and daring quests soon!

Any similarity to any actual dragons is purely coincidental. No Sir Sirs were harmed in the writing of this book. Covered in suds, yes. Maybe slightly frightened by Dragons they've only just met,. But not harmed. All bubbles filmed on location near Lake Roland, Maryland.

Made in the USA
Middletown, DE
06 August 2022